For Lionel Richard Sanders
Thank you for filling my childhood with tire swings, fishing
holes, and daily lessons of acceptance. Your constant
examples of compassion and zero tolerance for bullying
were the inspiration for this story.

ISBN-13: 978-0-9862-6210-4
Published by Little Lemon Production House
Written by Karen Sanders-Betts
Illustrated and Designed by Hannah Howerton
Copyright © 2015
MADE IN USA
Printed by Paul Baker Printing
www.thelittlelemonthatleapt.com
www.facebook.com/littlelemonbook
Twitter/Instagram: @littlelemonbook
#ichooseweird

MADE IN USA

PUBLISHED BY LITTLE LEMON PRODUCTION HOUSE

PRINTED BY

PAUL BAKER PRINTING

THE LITTLE LEMON THAT LEAPT

WRITTEN BY KAREN SANDERS-BETTS | ILLUSTRATED BY HANNAH HOWERTON

STARRING LIONEL THE LEMON

MOTHER/DAUGHTER ➡ AUTHOR/ILLUSTRATOR

Karen and Hannah are a mom-daughter duo from Northern California and the creative minds behind *The Little Lemon that Leapt*.

Karen (Mom/Writer) received her bachelor's degree in journalism and minor in English from The University of Central Missouri. Her lifelong dream of writing a children's book has finally come to fruition.

Hannah (Daughter/Illustrator) received her bachelor's degree in political science and minor in history of art from UC Berkeley, where she learned how wonderful weird really is.

With the help of Lionel the Lemon, Karen and Hannah hope to teach children to embrace their differences, while inciting some giggles along the way!

ENOUGH ABOUT YOU! LET'S START MY STORY!

They were **TOO BUSY** discussing more important things like **LEMON MERINGUE PIE,** **LEMON CURD,** and **LEMONADE.**

In other words...

THEIR DESTINIES!

The little lemon didn't join in on their curious conversations, or share their **DISTURBING DREAMS.**

From the tip top of the tree, the little lemon could **SEE THE WORLD.**

It was a

MAGNIFICENT,
MARVELOUS,
MESMERIZING
WORLD,

and the little lemon longed to be part of it.

He was deep in a daydream when a
BUMBLEBEE BUZZED BY
with a bundle of balloons and nearly
knocked him right off the tree.

"HEY, WATCH IT!"

the little lemon cried out.

"WAIT, WHERE ARE YOU GOING?"

The busy bee did not answer.
He had places to go. The little lemon
wanted to go places too.
He was sick of being stuck in a tree.

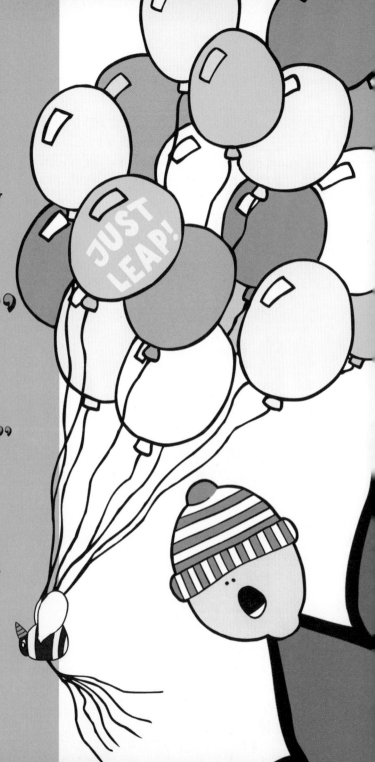

That is when he had (by far) his best idea of the day:

HE HAD TO LEAP!

His perfect plan had ONE teeny, tiny, tangle:

LEMONS. DON'T. LEAP.

Lemons hang and hover, they even dangle, droop, and drop;
BUT NEVER EVER, IN THE HISTORY OF TIME EVER,
had a lemon ever leapt.

LUCKILY,

the little lemon did not know this.

DIDN'T KNOW WHAT?

THE TREMENDOUS TREE SHOOK AND SWAYED

as the little lemon burst from its boughs
with a positively petrifying

POP!

WOO HOOOOO!

Dazed lemons by
the dozens watched with

DREAD and DISBELIEF

as the little lemon

LEAPT.

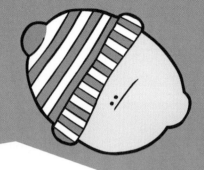

UH OH...I'M FEELING A BIT WOOZY

Pulling off a picture perfect landing, he gave the suitably shocked lemons a single salute and set off to

SEE the WORLD.

He hadn't gone far (not far at all) when he found himself head to head with a

HUFFY HEDGEHOG.

"**EXCUSE ME**,"
said the little lemon,
"WHAT ARE YOU DOING?"

The hedgehog HURRIEDLY hammered away.
"Hanging a banner for
my bluegrass band's
PREMIER PERFORMANCE,"
he replied.

The little lemon howled with laughter.
"Hedgehogs snuffle and snort, they even puff and pop,
but they DEFINITELY DON'T SING BLUEGRASS!"

He was still wondering about the weirdness of a singing hedgehog and a banjo banging bear when a

FIERY FLASH FILLED THE FOREST.

Bewildered by what it could be, the little lemon headed hastily toward the light.

THIS IS MY BEWILDERED FACE.

Through the trees, a **FASTIDIOUSLY FASHIONABLE FOX** was photographing a **RAKISH ROOSTER.**

"Excuse me, what are you doing?" asked the little lemon.

"I am taking a portrait of my **FINE FEATHERED FRIEND,**" the persnickety fox purred.

"Foxes can't be friends with roosters!" the little lemon said sassily.

"**FOXES EAT ROOSTERS!**"

"NOT THIS ONE," the fox said, GLARING over his glasses. "I am VERY much a vegan, and I LOVE LEMONADE. Care for a cup?"

FACE FLUSHED,

the little lemon took two steps back.

THE FOX QUICKLY FOLLOWED.

"NO?" HE QUIPPED.

"Then I suggest that you GO AWAY."

So for the second time that day, the little lemon **(QUITE QUICKLY)** went away.

"I AM PROPERLY PACKED AND PREPARING TO **FLY** TO **PARIS** FOR CULINARY CLASSES," the penguin pompously replied.

THIS DAY JUST GOT A 'LATTE' WEIRDER.

Gasping through giggles, **THE LITTLE LEMON** finally found his voice;

"**PENGUINS CAN'T COOK! HEY, PENGUINS CAN'T EVEN FLY!**"

"THIS ONE CAN!" the perturbed penguin **BARKED BACK** as he boarded his flight to France. **"I have sauces to study. NOW GO AWAY!"**

GOOD LUCK ON THE MACARONS!

For the third time that day, the little lemon (SOMEWHAT SOURLY)

WENT AWAY.

"What a weird world,"

he said to himself.

HEY! A DIME!

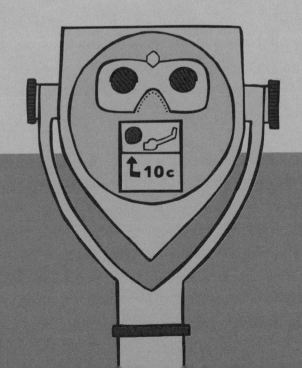

It wasn't long, not long at all, before he stumbled upon a

CURIOUS CONTRAPTION.

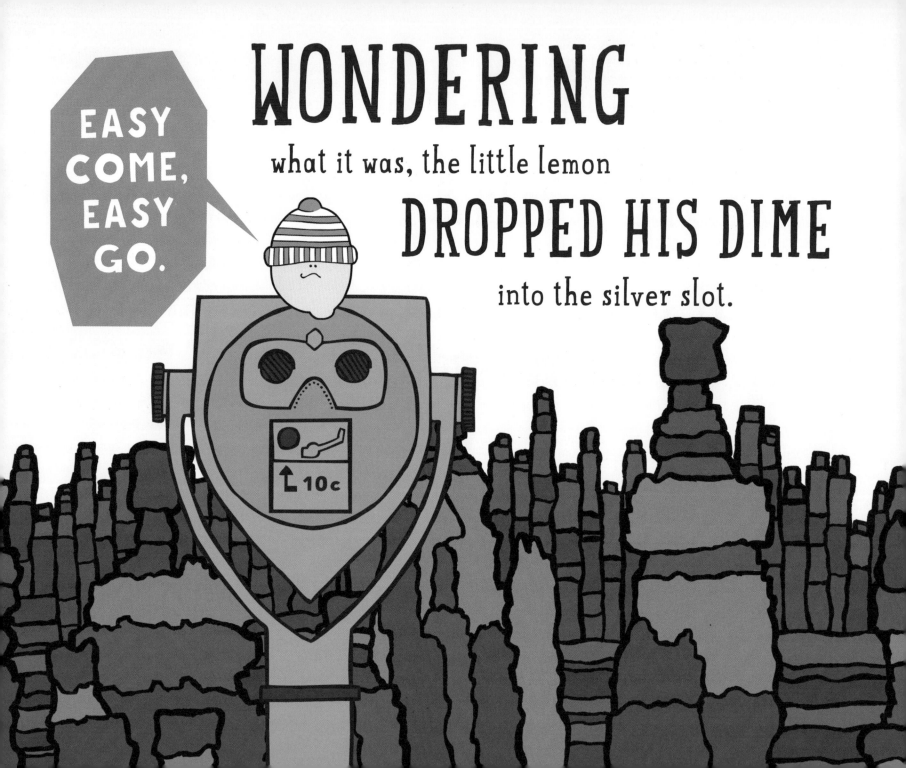

"WHAT ARE YOU DOING UP THERE?" the little lemon bellowed.

"CLIMBING TO THE CREST!"

the sporty sloth bellowed back.

Lesson STILL not learned, the little lemon's laughter echoed up the rugged rocks.

"SLOTHS DON'T CLIMB ROCKS!" he called out.
"SLOTHS BARELY EVEN BUDGE!"

"THIS ONE DOES!" the scaling sloth snapped.
"I AM CLEARLY CONCENTRATING. NOW GO AWAY!"
So for the fourth time that day,
the little lemon (rather reluctantly) went away.

ALTHOUGH I SURE COULD USE A COLD CUP OF LEMONADE...

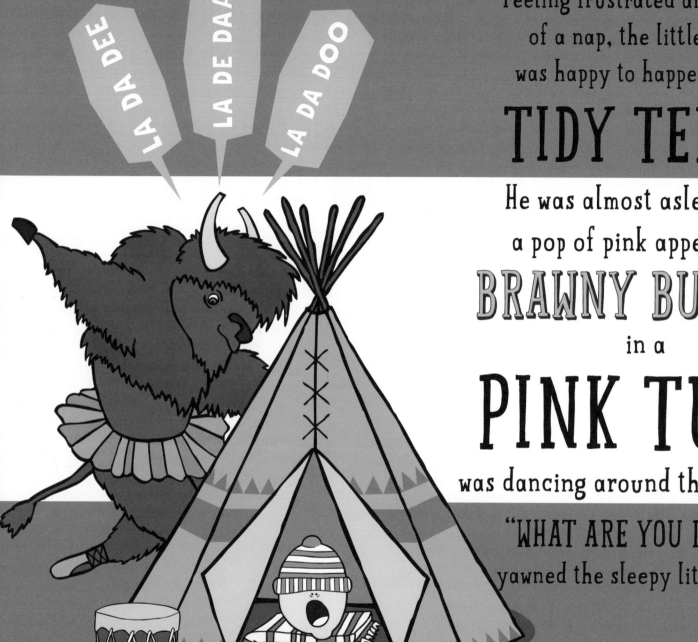

Feeling frustrated and in need of a nap, the little lemon was happy to happen upon a

TIDY TEPEE.

He was almost asleep when a pop of pink appeared. A

BRAWNY BUFFALO

in a

PINK TUTU

was dancing around the tiny tepee!

"WHAT ARE YOU DOING?" yawned the sleepy little lemon.

TWIRLING AS HE TALKED,
the buffalo briskly replied,
"PRACTICING MY PIROUETTES!"

SNORT HUFF GRUNT

This gave the little lemon (by far)
his BIGGEST laugh of the day.
"Buffaloes don't dance,
and ballet is for GIRLS!"

The big bull stopped spinning.
"THIS ONE DOES, BEANIE BOY!"

chased (of course) by the big bull
buffalo in his petal pink tutu
as the world whirled by.

THIS BEANIE WAS BUILT
FOR SPEED!

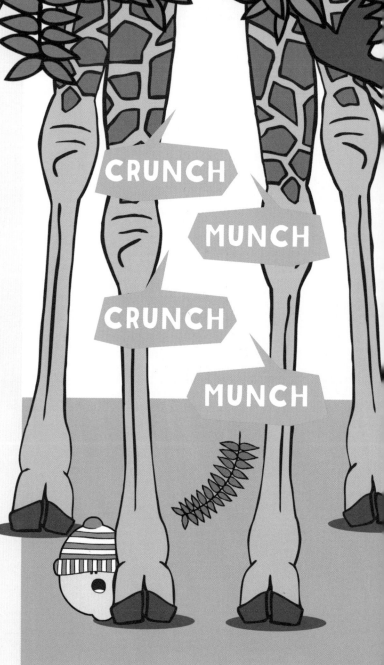

HE RAN (AND HE RAN) UNTIL HE RAN

right into the long leg of a

GINORMOUS GIRAFFE.

The little lemon looked high into the sky.

"WHAT ARE YOU DOING UP THERE?"

he hollered.

The ginormous giraffe

CRUNCHED AND MUNCHED.

"Enjoying a leisurely lunch,"
he said briefly between bites.

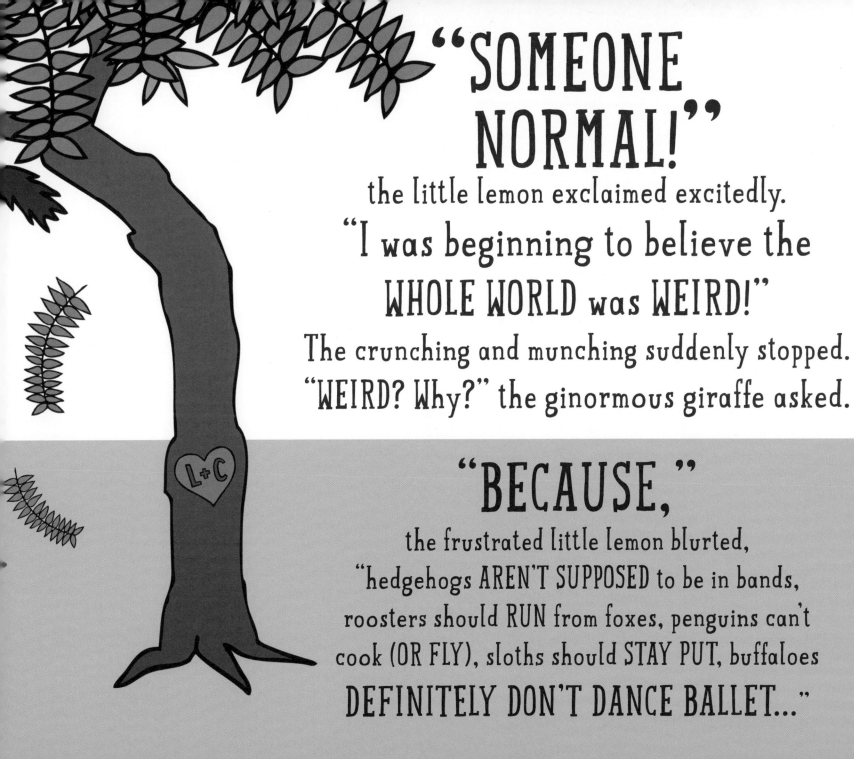

"SOMEONE NORMAL!"
the little lemon exclaimed excitedly.
"I was beginning to believe the
WHOLE WORLD was WEIRD!"
The crunching and munching suddenly stopped.
"WEIRD? Why?" the ginormous giraffe asked.

"BECAUSE,"
the frustrated little lemon blurted,
"hedgehogs AREN'T SUPPOSED to be in bands,
roosters should RUN from foxes, penguins can't
cook (OR FLY), sloths should STAY PUT, buffaloes
DEFINITELY DON'T DANCE BALLET..."

The ginormous giraffe gently interjected:
"And lemons don't leap."

"YEAH,"
the little lemon almost agreed,
"and lemons don't...wait,
WHAT?"

The little lemon looked a
WEE BIT WORRIED
"This one did," he said hesitantly.
"Does that make ME weird?"

THE GINORMOUS GIRAFFE

swiftly swooped to the little lemon's level.

"ABSOLUTELY!"

he said with a wise wink, "and weird is (by far) my favorite."

For the first time that day, the little lemon saw what makes the world

MAGNIFICENT, MARVELOUS, AND MESMERIZING.

Everyone is a little bit weird, and THAT is what makes them wonderful.

The ginormous giraffe nudged his new friend.

"Do you want to go back to the tree, or would you rather

EXPLORE

the rest of this

WEIRD WORLD?"

OH BOY.

DO GIRAFFES USUALLY HAVE MUSTACHES?

Lesson learned,
the little lemon smiled.

"I CHOOSE WEIRD!"

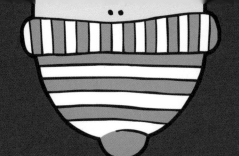

THE
END

#ichooseweird

THANK YOU FOR BELIEVING!

Aleena, Natasha & Keira
The Anapolsky Family
Gregory Andrews
Laird Jacob Baradat
Gulay Bayramoglu
David Betts
Dr. & Mrs. Stanley Betts
Brent & Ina Booth
The Brousseau Family
Dr. & Mrs. Bassett Brown
Vicki Polster & Chuck Cech
Dorothy Compeau
Chad Douglas
Ellie Drue
Mark & Kelly Epperson
Logan & Gavin Flores
Vance & Terralee Ginther
Hannibal High School Class of 1983
Stefanie Kelly
The Keppner Family
Jay, Jean, & Elijah Kim
Jeanie Knight
Eddie Lehman
Chris McAllister
The Scott McAllister Family

Tom & Mary Jo McAllister
Wilbur & Beverly McSorley
Maxwell Roger Lee & Jackson Miles
Rose Nemes-Oslica
The Northcutt Family
The Patmon Family
Coleman & Gabrielle Reavey
Robert Regan
The Rhines Family
The Brett Rosenthal Family
Marcus, Kim, Xander & Aiden Rosenthal
Ivy Rylander
Sac State's Speech Pathology Department
Kylor Richard Sanders
Lionel Richard & Carole Sanders
Jonathan Sherwood & Lance Schnell
Dick & Wilma Serns
Amelia Silva-Snow
The Sproul Family
Tom & June Stephens
The Grandchildren of James & Joyce Teel
Madison & Mackenzie Terry
Miki Teixeira
The Ross Walden Family
The Witzke Family